Oliver Moon and the Troll Trouble

Sue Mongredien

Illustrated by

Jan McCafferty

USBORNE

For Tom Powell,
who thought of the title

First published in 2008 by Usborne Publishing Ltd., Usborne House,
83-85 Saffron Hill, London EC1N 8RT, England. www.usborne.com

Text copyright © Sue Mongredien Ltd., 2008

Illustration copyright © Usborne Publishing Ltd., 2008

A CIP catalogue record for this book is available from
the British Library.

JFMAMJJAS ND/08   ISBN 9780746086865

Printed in Great Britain.

Contents

Chapter One   7

Chapter Two   22

Chapter Three   36

Chapter Four   51

Chapter Five   67

Chapter Six   76

Chapter Seven   82

Chapter One

"Have a nice day at Magic School, Oliver," Mrs. Moon called, waving him off from the front doorstep. "And good luck in the audition!"

"Good 'uck!" Oliver's little sister, the Witch Baby, echoed, beaming at him.

"Thanks," Oliver said. His school was putting on a play, *Monstrous Magic*, in a few weeks' time, and today was the day that all the students got to try out for various roles. "See you later!"

Jake Frogfreckle, Oliver's best friend, was waiting at the corner of the road. "Hi, Oliver," he said with a nervous grin. "All ready for the audition?"

"I think so," Oliver said, a fluttering feeling starting up in his tummy. "I hope I get picked for a part – especially as one of the heroes. How about you?"

Jake nodded. "Me too," he said. "I'm wearing my lucky socks, my lucky vest *and* I've got a lucky charm with me." He opened his bag to show Oliver a dried toad on a key ring.

"Oh," Oliver said. "I didn't think of that. I haven't got any lucky stuff with me today." He bit his lip. It was too late to turn back for home and grab something now.

The two young wizards walked along together, both thinking about the play.

In a school assembly last week, their
head teacher, Mrs. MacLizard, had told
them all about it. She'd said it was about
two brave wizards, Mortimer and
Oswald, who entered a world of
monsters in an attempt to
find a lost spell book. On
their journey, the heroes
met friendly firework
sprites, naughty goblins,
funny sea
monsters, a
tribe of warrior
wizards and even a
scary troll. "So there
really is something
for everyone," she had
finished by saying.

"We'll have costumes, magic, dancing and drama. It's going to be a wonderful show!"

Oliver couldn't help daydreaming of himself and Jake being Mortimer and Oswald, the heroes of the show, taking their bows onstage to thunderous applause and cheers from the audience. Lucky charm or no lucky charm, he couldn't wait for the auditions to begin!

When it was time for Oliver's class to audition for the play, they trooped into the main hall. Mrs. MacLizard was waiting for them there, along with Ms. Darling, the drama teacher. Ms. Darling had tumbling red curls which she liked tossing over her shoulders in a dramatic fashion, and wore a long green velvet cloak and bright purple high heels.

"Welcome, welcome!" she gushed. "Come in, come in. I'm thrilled to see so many budding actors and actresses here today! Thrilled!"

Some of the girls, like Hattie Toadtrumper and Pippi Prowlcat, smiled shyly at Ms. Darling, but Oliver saw Bully Bogeywort rolling his eyes and pretending to be sick at the back of the room.

"Now, I'll give you all a page or two from the script," she said, and waved her wand. A pile of papers flew up into the air and separated gracefully, like a flock of birds, before flying down, one each, to everyone. "And then we'll do some group readings to see how you get on.

If you could form groups of four, please?"

Jake and Oliver stood together and called Colin Cockroach over to join them. Now they just needed one more person to make up their foursome. Oliver looked around hopefully. Hattie, Pippi, Lucy Lizardlegs and Carly Catstail were already bunched together as one group.

"How about Mitch or Harvey?" Oliver suggested, moving towards them. Too late – they had just joined up with Boris Batbottom and Eric Earwax.

In fact, Oliver thought, as he looked around the room, everyone seemed to be in groups of four already, except...

Oh, great.

Except for Bully Bogeywort, the most

horrible boy in Magic School. Obviously nobody wanted to be with *him*!

"Right – you four boys can go together," Ms. Darling said, coming over just then, and motioning them towards one another. Then she spoke to the whole class. "Rehearse in your groups for five minutes, then show me your acting talents. The scene I've given you comes just after the two heroes have escaped from the dangerous forest troll. I take it you know about trolls?"

"Yes, Miss," Pippi said with a shudder. "They are very scary and they eat people, don't they?"

Ms. Darling nodded. "That's right," she replied. "So, how do you think Mortimer and Oswald are feeling here, having just escaped from one?"

"Scared," suggested Eric.

"Relieved," said Carly.

"Their hearts will be pounding!" added Hattie.

"Absolutely," Ms. Darling said. "Off you go, then. Have fun!"

The air buzzed with excited voices as everyone began the task. Oliver glanced down at his paper. The scene involved the two heroes Mortimer and Oswald, and two evil witches.

"Right, I'll be Mortimer and Colin can be Oswald," Bully said in a bossy voice. "You two can be the witches."

Bristling with annoyance – why did Bully always have to take over everything? – Oliver turned to Jake. "Do you want to be Bella or Donna?"

Jake shrugged. "Bella?" he said, looking like he didn't care.

"Fine," Oliver said. "Okay, let's try it out."

The four of them studied the script. The first thing on the page was a set of stage directions which said: *A cold, dark wood. Mortimer and Oswald stumble their way through, tripping on tree roots as they go.*

Mortimer – played by Bully – was first to speak. "Where are we?" he said, treading gingerly along the floor and pretending to shiver.

"In the hall, of course," Colin replied, staring at Bully as if he were mad.

"No, bat-brain! We're reading the play now!" Bully snapped as Oliver and Jake both tried not to laugh. Bully jabbed at his script. "See there, where it says *Oswald*? That's your line, that is. Got it?"

"Got it," Colin said.

There was a pause.

"Well, go on, then, read it!" Bully ordered.

Colin looked up, a wounded expression on his face. "I *am* reading it," he protested. "Oh – you mean *out loud*? Oh, right."

"Maybe we should start again," Oliver suggested, noticing Colin turning pink around the ears.

"All right," Bully grumbled. Then he did his pretend-shivering act again. "Where are we?" he asked, stumbling along.

"I don't know, but…" Colin squinted at his script. "Oh, I need my new glasses to read this," he said glumly. "I can't see it very well."

Ms. Darling clapped her hands. "That's enough rehearsal time," she said. "Let's see what you can do!"

Oliver, Jake, Bully and Colin fell silent and stared at each other. Enough rehearsal time? They hadn't even got further than two lines of speech!

"This is going to be a disaster," Oliver muttered to Jake. "We're doomed!"

Chapter Two

"Let's see…" Ms. Darling gazed around the room. "Boys, you can go first!"

Oliver felt tense as the rest of the class turned to watch.

"Off you go, then," Ms. Darling prompted. "And…ACTION!"

Bully launched into his pretend shivering. "Brrrr…" he said. "Where are we?"

Colin stared at his script, holding it so close to his face that it was practically pressed against his nose. "I don't know," he said, his voice coming out very muffled through the paper. "Far from that awful troll, I hope!"

Someone giggled from the crowd, and Colin's neck turned red.

"I've never been so terrified," Bully read aloud. "I thought he was going to bite my head off when he swiped at me like that!"

Colin peered at his script again. "Look, there's a house over there," he read. "Let's knock and ask for shelter."

Bully mimed walking along and knocking on a door just as Colin mimed walking along and knocking on a *different* door two metres behind him.

There were another couple of giggles, and Ms. Darling narrowed her eyes.

"Oi! Colin! *This* is the door!" Bully hissed.

Colin was still knocking on his patch of air, shaking his head stubbornly. "This is *my* door," he retorted.

This time even Mrs. MacLizard let out a chuckle. "What a double act!" she wheezed.

Bella opens the door of the witches' cottage, Oliver read from the script. Ahh. Was he Bella or Donna? He couldn't remember. He scuttled over and pretended to open Bully's imaginary door – just as he saw Jake opening Colin's one. Oh, right. It looked like Jake was Bella, after all!

"Greetings," Jake read out in a cackling sort of voice. "And what brings you out on such a blustery night?"

There was a pause. "Ooh, sorry. Is it me?" Colin gulped, bringing the paper up to his face again – and everyone burst out laughing, Ms. Darling included.

"Oh dear," she chuckled. "Maybe you needed a bit more time, boys. Never mind. That was very funny, I have to say, even if it wasn't intended that way. Perhaps I'll put you down for some of the comedy parts."

Oliver stared as she scribbled some notes on her clipboard and turned away. Was that *it*? "Ms. Darling, um…I haven't actually said anything yet…" he began, but she was already talking to Hattie's group.

"Girls," she said. "I hope you're going to give us a more *polished* performance than we've just seen?"

Oliver's shoulders slumped. Great. So his chance to audition was over, was it? Ruined by Colin and Bully! He'd never be chosen for one of the heroes now. Maybe he wouldn't even get a part at all! He might as well forget the whole thing.

At the end of that day, Oliver's class were packing away the equipment from their

Enchanted Art lesson, when the blackboard started rippling and shimmering all different colours.

"Sir, sir!" Hattie squeaked excitedly, pointing at it. "Something weird is happening!"

Everyone stared, including Mr. Goosepimple, the teacher. Suddenly the board glowed a deep green, and then black letters appeared on it, as if an invisible hand was writing there.

"Cast list for *Monstrous Magic*," Mr. Goosepimple read aloud. "Ooh!" he exclaimed. "That was quick. They've decided on the roles already!"

Oliver held his breath, wishing he'd thought to bring along a lucky charm today, like Jake. Anything would help!

Cast list for
Monstrous Magic

He crossed his fingers hopefully. He knew his audition hadn't gone well, but could there still be a tiny chance that Ms. Darling had thought he *looked* worthy of playing a hero?

There was a hush as new words appeared on the board.

Mortimer — Merlin Spoonbender

Oswald — Arthur Silvertongue

"Surprise, surprise," Jake muttered, his eyes glued to the board. "I *knew* they'd pick prefects for the best parts."

More names rolled up — all older wizards and witches for the main roles of the play. But then...

Firework sprites:

Eliza Evil-eyes

Chloe Cloaksmith

Hattie Toadtrumper

Pippi Prowlcat

"Yessss!" Pippi squealed, doing high fives with Hattie.

"We're in the play!" Hattie screeched, beaming broadly.

There were a few congratulations and then the list of firework sprites vanished.

Oliver stared at the blackboard, wondering what the magic writing would spell next. How he hoped *he'd* get something in the play, too!

Then came the list of the warrior wizards, in curling black letters. Oliver crossed his fingers. The warrior wizards sounded cool – fighting *and* magic to perform onstage.

Warrior wizards:

Horace Hogsbody

Ricky Ravenbeak

Jake Frogfreckle

"No way!" Jake cheered, punching the air in delight.

Pedro Pumpkinseed

Eric Earwax

Will Whiskerchin

The writing stopped, and Oliver let out his breath in disappointment. He'd have loved to have been picked to be a warrior wizard with Jake!

He managed to force a smile for his friend's sake. "Nice one," he said, as Jake

exchanged grins and thumbs-up signs
with Horace and Eric.

More magic writing appeared, this
time to say that Bully and Colin had
been given the comedy roles of the
naughty goblins.

Then, Lucy and Carly were cast as bats, and a load of other people from the class were included in the elf chorus.

Oliver's cheeks burned. Was he really the only one without a part? All his friends were whispering excitedly about costumes and lines and dance routines and songs to learn. He'd been forgotten, it seemed. Typical!

Then, just as he thought the magic writing had come to an end, a new line appeared on the board. Oliver read the words and his mouth fell open in dismay.

Troll – Oliver Moon, it said.

Chapter Three

Troll. *Troll!* He'd been cast as the horrible, dangerous forest troll! Not a hero – not even a good guy. The troll, who tried to bite Mortimer's head off! He'd be booed, not clapped by the audience!

Bully, of course, was roaring with laughter and Oliver felt himself grow hot with embarrassment as a couple of other people giggled.

Play scripts suddenly appeared in the air and floated down, one landing on each student's desk. Oliver flicked through his, trying his hardest not to be too downcast. You never could tell – the troll might have a few good jokes, or a dramatic scene somewhere in the play...

He found the troll scene on page forty. Oh, right. All the troll seemed to do was snore and scratch itself, grunt and roar. That was it.

Oliver's cheeks flamed even hotter. Now he wished he hadn't been given a part at all!

Luckily, the bell rang for the end of school just then. Oliver stuffed the script in his cloak pocket and rushed out as fast as he could.

"Well?" his mum wanted to know as soon as he walked through the front door. "How did it go? Did you get picked for anything in the play?"

"Yes," Oliver said, kicking off his shoes and hanging up his cloak.

"Oh my goodness!" Mrs. Moon screamed, hugging and kissing him in excitement. "That's brilliant! Oh, we'll have to get tickets for everyone. A part in the play – just wait till I tell Granny Moon and…" She stopped. "Oliver, what's wrong? You don't look very happy."

"I'm not," Oliver growled. "I've been given the part of the troll, that's why.

The rotten old grunting troll. And I wanted to be a hero!"

"Grunt, grunt," the Witch Baby put in helpfully, toddling through from the living room.

"Exactly," Oliver sighed. "Grunt, grunt."

His mum put an arm around him.

"Well…" She faltered. Then she gave him a big squeeze. "Well, you're still *my* hero. You'll be the best troll ever, I bet." She ruffled his hair. "Come into the kitchen. Your sister and I have been baking a snake cake – I'll cut you a slice. That'll make you feel better."

Unfortunately, even after two large slabs of snake cake and a nice cool drink of slug juice, Oliver didn't feel better  at all. In fact, he felt worse.

"I think I might tell Ms. Darling I don't want to be in the play," he said to his dad, who had just got home from work.

Mr. Moon gave him a hug. "That would be a shame," he said. "Especially as I know you were looking forward to it. I mean, I know trolls are a bit…" He shuddered. "…Well, a bit horrible, but it'll still be fun to act in the play."

"It won't be fun," Oliver said, his shoulders slumped. "What's fun about being a troll?"

"Well…" His dad paused. "Trolls are quite interesting creatures, you know," he went on. "Why don't we find out a bit more about them before you make your mind up? We could look on the Wizard Wide Web, if you like."

Oliver shrugged, not feeling like he cared very much, but his dad led him to the far corner of the living room, where

they kept their Web, and tapped it
with his wand. "We need to find out
everything about trolls, please," he said.

Oliver watched as the Web made a
faint crackling sound, then a picture of
a troll's face appeared in the middle.

"This is a troll," said an official-sounding voice. "Trolls are large creatures, with many warts, enormous feet and a distinctive smell."

A puff of green smoke wafted from the Web just then, and Oliver and his dad both recoiled, clutching their noses.

"Pooo!" Oliver choked, gagging on the stench.

"That is *bad*," his dad agreed, fanning the air in front of his face. "Phew-eee!"

"Trolls eat anything," the voice continued. "Animals, people, trees, plants – even stones, if they are really hungry."

A new picture appeared on the screen, of a troll biting happily into a rock. One of his big brown teeth fell out, but he didn't seem to notice. Oliver winced.

Ouch! he thought. The troll had to be seriously tough not to have noticed his own tooth coming out.

"Trolls live in dark forests," the voice went on. "They rarely venture out of their natural habitat, for they have no sense of direction and get lost very easily. This is because of their tiny little brains."

"Granny Moon said a troll once came into Cacklewick," Mr. Moon said. "But that was about two hundred years ago."

"Really? Wow!" Oliver said. "What happened?"

"I think it just ate a few people and found its way back again," Mr. Moon said. "And—"

"Excuse me!" barked the voice from the web. "Pay attention! I'm trying to tell you about trolls!"

Oliver and his dad exchanged glances. "Sorry," Oliver said politely. "We're listening now."

"Trolls are slow-witted creatures, and often have strange thought patterns," the voice went on. "For instance, if a troll can't see for any reason, they think it's night-time and fall asleep at once."

Mr. Moon chuckled. "Unbelievable!" he said.

"That *is* quite funny," Oliver admitted.

"Despite their thick skins, trolls are sensitive creatures," the voice said next. "They don't like being laughed at or teased, and are likely to fly into a rage if they think somebody is being rude to them. That is why the Witch and Wizard

Health and Safety Board advise all witches and wizards to stay well away from trolls."

Oliver watched as a new picture appeared, of a troll picking up a huge boulder and hurling it to the ground in anger. "Remind me never to be rude to a troll," he said nervously.

"Finally, a brief guide to troll noises," the voice said. Then there came a loud snuffling sound. **SNORT SNORT SNUFFLE!**

"This is a troll hunting for food," said the voice.

GRRRRR! GRRRRUNT! GRUNT GRUNT GRUNT!

"This is the sound of an angry troll," the voice said.

ROARRRRR! GRRRRRRR! ROARRRRR!

"And that is the sound of a troll about to attack," said the voice. "For more detailed information on trolls, you can visit Trolls.com. This Fact File was prepared by the Wizard Broadcasting Company. Thank you and goodbye."

The Web crackled and the picture faded away.

"Grunt, grunt!" the Witch Baby said just then, pulling a horrible face and pretending to chew the table leg. "Me a troll! Grunt, grunt!"

"I wish *I* wasn't," Oliver said, slumping onto the sofa.

Chapter Four

"Marvellous, darlings!" Ms. Darling trilled. "Let's take it from the top of scene three again!"

One week later, rehearsals were well under way for *Monstrous Magic*. By now, Oliver had perfected a really excellent troll roar that made some of the cast members actually scream in fear.

He could make everyone else laugh, with
his loud troll snore. Okay, so it wasn't
the heroic part he'd hoped for – but
he did rather enjoy making people giggle.

Oliver's classmates were having fun
with the play, too. Jake and the rest of
the warrior wizards had been practising
their fight routine endlessly. Hattie and

Pippi had spent hours rehearsing their firework sprite dance, and Bully and Colin were polishing up their double act as the cheeky goblins, and being surprisingly funny with it.

Other Magic School students were hard at work with costumes, scenery and props for the play. The whole school was involved, it seemed.

"It's going to be a fabulous show," Ms. Darling said happily at the end of that evening's rehearsal. "Now, I need a quick word with the props people, please, so if they could all stay behind? Everyone else, you can go. Don't dawdle – it looks like there's going to be a storm. Thank you!"

Oliver left the hall with Jake and the others, and went to get his cloak. Then he remembered he'd left his bag in the hall, on the stage. "I'll see you tomorrow," he told Jake. "I've just got to go back to get my bag."

Oliver went along the corridor on his own. Out of the window, he could see a small copse of trees next to the playground where the Magic School students often played Hide and Shriek. Dark thunderclouds were massing behind them, and a wind was blowing leaves around the ground. A strange smell was carried through an open window on the breeze and Oliver wrinkled his nose. He was sure he'd smelled it before. An earthy, mouldy sort of smell, as if something had been left to rot for a hundred years or so…

The door of the school hall had been left slightly open and as Oliver approached, he could hear Ms. Darling's loud, high voice floating through. "…And please can we have the troll costume as ugly as possible? Let's have a truly hideous troll to frighten the audience!"

"**GRUNT!**"

Oliver stopped walking in surprise.
Where had that grunt come from?
Was someone making troll noises at him?
He looked around but there was nobody
else in the corridor. It had started to rain
now, and a flurry of drops lashed against
the window.

"...So I was thinking, great big brown teeth – ugh! – and thick lumpy feet covered in yucky warts," Ms. Darling went on brightly. "And lots of horrible matted fur on the troll's body, of course. As if the filthy thing hadn't ever washed itself!"

"**GRRRRR! GRUNT GRUNT!**"

Oliver looked round again. The sound was nearer but the corridor was still empty. He looked out of the window – and his eyes widened in shock. There, stomping along the edge of the playground through the pouring rain, was a huge creature. It was covered in shaggy hair. It had big brown teeth. It had thick, lumpy, warty feet. Its arms swung by its sides, its eyes blazed with an angry light, and its footsteps made the ground shake. The strange smell had become much stronger now, choking and foul.

Oliver thought his heart was almost going to burst with fright. It was a troll! A real troll, right there at Magic School!

"…And it would be great if you could have some kind of disgusting troll *smell* wafting around," Ms. Darling was saying. "I've never smelled one myself but apparently they really pong!"

Oliver couldn't take his eyes off the troll. It seemed to have heard everything Ms. Darling had just said. With a huge roar of rage, the troll ripped up a tree with one hand, swung it up over its head and smashed it down on the ground.

CRASH!

The tree thumped down with such a *thwack* that the school building shook, and several windows smashed. Oliver heard screams from the hall. "What was *that*?" someone shouted.

There was a great thunderclap then, and a flash of lightning. This seemed to frighten the troll because it turned and ran, its great legs striding across the ground into the distance.

Oliver dashed into the hall, his heart thudding. "Did you see it? Did you see the troll?" he panted.

The props people and Ms. Darling were staring at the shattered glass all over the floor from the broken windows. At Oliver's words, they swung round in alarm. "The what?" one of the props wizards replied. "What troll?"

"Outside," Oliver said, pointing to the window. "It was right out there!"

There was a shocked silence. Then Ms. Darling started to clap. "Oh, Oliver!" she said, smiling broadly. "You had us all going there!"

Oliver felt taken aback. Didn't she believe him? "But I saw it," he insisted. "With my own eyes! A real troll – I'm not making it up!"

Ms. Darling pointed her wand at the broken glass on the floor, and all the pieces jumped back into the window frame, melting together to form clear panes once more.

"Very funny," she said. "But I think we all know what thunder sounds like. Besides, trolls don't come out of their forest homes, do they? With all your research, I thought you'd know that by now."

A couple of the props wizards had gone to the window and were staring out. "There's a fallen tree, Miss," one of them said.

"The troll pulled it up," Oliver said. "It just ripped it out of the ground. Honestly! I think it must have heard you saying mean things about trolls, and—"

An irritated note came into Ms. Darling's voice. "Oliver, a joke's a joke," she said. "But it's not funny any more, all right?"

"But the tree—" he began.

She interrupted him. "Well, that was the lightning, of course," she said. "Must have struck it, to knock it over like that."

Oliver let out a sigh of frustration. Why wouldn't she believe him? He was telling the truth! "But Miss—" he tried a final time.

"Oliver Moon, that's enough!" she snapped. "For goodness' sake! Perhaps you've spent too long thinking about being a troll. You're starting to imagine real ones now."

Someone giggled nervously, and Oliver turned red. He knew what he'd seen! But how could he make Ms. Darling believe him?

There was another rumble of thunder

from outside. The rain was absolutely pouring by now. "I think I'd better send everyone straight home," Ms. Darling said. "I don't want any of you walking back in this weather."

Oliver couldn't help a nervous glance out of the window. There was no sign of anything out there now, except the rain. "Shouldn't we just check?" he asked. "Or call for the police wizards, or something? If there's a troll loose in Cacklewick, then…"

But Ms. Darling was already swirling her wand around through the air. "Blow, wind, blow. Home we must go!" she commanded.

There was a sizzling sound from her wand, and a few blue crackles sputtered from its tip. Then Oliver felt himself rushing through the air, with the school and everything else a blur before his eyes.

Chapter Five

Oliver was half-expecting to go to
school the next day and see that *all* the
trees had been ripped out by the angry
troll, but there was no sign it had been
back. In fact, there was no sign a troll
had been there at all, now that the fallen
tree had been taken away by the
caretaker wizard.

Oliver hadn't mentioned the troll to his parents and sister. Once he'd got home, the whole thing had seemed so crazy, he'd started to wonder if he really *had* imagined it, as Ms. Darling had suggested. Had he been thinking so much about trolls, he'd actually dreamed one up? Perhaps it *had* been lightning that had knocked the tree to the ground…

Whatever had happened, life at Magic School seemed completely normal now. If it *had* been a troll, it seemed to have gone back to wherever it had come from. All the same, Oliver couldn't help thinking back to that dark and stormy night every now and then, and glancing out of the window. Just to be on the safe side…

*

A week of frantic rehearsals later, and it was the opening night of the show. Oliver felt very excited as he pulled on his big hairy troll costume. "Good luck, everyone," Ms. Darling said to the  cast as they waited backstage. "I'm sure you'll all be fabulous. And I've just heard a rumour that there's a reviewer from *The Cacklewick Chronicle* in the audience tonight. So do your best! Make Magic School proud!"

There was a round of gasps at her

words. *The Cacklewick Chronicle* was the local newspaper and *everyone* read it. Oliver grinned, imagining the excitement of seeing a review of the play in black and white. Maybe even some photos…

"I don't know what *you're* looking so excited about," Bully Bogeywort hissed meanly to Oliver. "They're not gonna print any photos of a *troll*!"

Oliver glared, but before he could reply, Ms. Darling was shushing everyone. "Curtain up!" she whispered.

Oliver crossed his fingers as the curtains opened, and Merlin Spoonbender and Arthur Silvertongue, in costume as Mortimer and Oswald, stepped out onto the stage and spoke their first lines. The show had begun!

Soon afterwards, the warrior wizards had to go on and perform their fight routine, which went very well, and had everyone clapping at the end. The audience seemed to be thoroughly enjoying themselves, laughing, gasping and cheering in all the right places.

The time soon came for Oliver to make his first appearance. He stomped onto the stage, crushing stink bombs between his fingers to make a suitably mouldy troll smell.

"Poo! Ugh!" squealed the audience.

"You smelly, Ollie!" he heard the Witch Baby giggle.

"GRRRRR!" went Oliver in his best troll imitation. "ROAR! GRRRR!"

"What is this foul, stinky beast?" cried

Mortimer (a magnificently moustached Merlin).

"Such an ugly brute!" said Oswald (a red tunicked Arthur). "I say we fight!"

This was Oliver's cue to advance on the heroes, roaring and grunting for all he was worth. But before he could move one of his big lumpy troll feet, he heard great stamping footsteps behind him.

STAMP, STAMP, STAMP!

"Ooh – a second troll!" someone from the audience marvelled.

"And it's even smellier!" another person commented.

Merlin gave a terrified shout. Arthur backed away to hide behind the scenery, his face very pale beneath his make-up.

Oliver swung round – which was quite difficult in his big costume – and froze to the spot with fright. There *was* a second troll onstage. But it wasn't a troll

in a costume, like him. It was a real one.
The one he'd seen before.

The troll was back!

Chapter Six

Oliver stared in horror at the shambling creature as it stomped towards him. "Them laugh at trolls," it muttered in a low, rumbling voice. "Them rude. I punish." The troll grabbed a cardboard tree from the scenery and stuffed it into its mouth, chomping it up with its huge teeth. Then it gave a threatening roar at the audience.

Oliver gulped. *I punish?* That sounded
scary beyond words. What was the troll
going to sink its teeth into next?

He backed away slowly, his heart
racing. What should he do? Could he run
fast enough in his costume?

Behind him, he could hear Merlin whimpering. "Don't eat us!" he begged. Arthur, meanwhile, had started crying in fear.

The audience had gone deathly quiet now. Then Oliver heard an old witch whisper, "What's going on? Is this meant to be happening?"

"No," Ms. Darling said hoarsely. "That's actually a real troll."

A scream went up. "A troll! A real troll! Run for your lives!"

Witches and wizards got to their feet, but the troll swung round to face the audience, shaking his fist. "You stay," he said, then plucked up a young wizard boy from the front row. "Or I eat HIM."

A gasp went around the room. The little wizard boy began to cry. Oliver felt sick with fright. He couldn't let the troll eat the little wizard! No way! But what could he do to stop it?

Then something clicked in Oliver's mind. The Web… What was it he'd heard on the Web about trolls falling asleep?

If a troll can't see for any reason, they think it's night-time and fall asleep at once…

Maybe that was the solution! But how was he going to cover the troll's eyes? If he went anywhere near it, it was sure to attack him!

His gaze fell upon the curtain at the side of the stage. That would have to do! He yanked it off its rail with a loud *rrrrrriipp!*

"Be careful, Oliver!" Ms. Darling wailed, wringing her hands as the troll turned towards Oliver at the noise.

Oliver's heart thumped as the troll grunted suspiciously and took a step towards him, still clutching the little wizard. Oliver took a deep breath. It was now or never. He had to act!

Chapter Seven

Using all his strength, Oliver jumped up and threw the curtain over the troll's head. He held his breath as the curtain material settled over the troll's eyes and nose and then...

ZZZZZZZZZZZZZZZZZZZ!

A tremendous snoring started up from underneath the curtain.

Oliver held his breath, almost not
daring to believe his luck. It had worked
– the troll had actually fallen asleep!

The audience were still silent,
seemingly stunned with fear. The little
wizard wriggled out of the troll's arms
and ran back to his mummy.

Then Oliver pulled off his troll mask, just in case anyone in the audience was at all worried that *he* was a real troll too. "I think we're safe now," he said. "The troll's asleep."

Ms. Darling ran onstage and hugged Oliver. "This brave young wizard has just saved us all!" she cried dramatically.

Oliver did a little bow, which was quite tricky in his costume. Then Ms. Darling dropped her voice to a stage whisper, remembering to be quiet. "I'm sorry for the interruption to our show," she hissed to the audience. "But could someone please summon the police wizards to take this troll away?"

A witch in the front row stood up and swished her wand through the air. Immediately, five police wizards appeared onstage, with bright red power-wands and red pointy hats on their heads. They chanted a spell in solemn voices, turning their wands in a complicated pattern as they did so. Red sparkles crackled from the ends of their wands, surrounding the curtain-covered troll, who was still snoring.

The sparkles circled the troll, then dissolved into a thick red mist. As the mist cleared, Oliver gaped in surprise. The troll had vanished – with only the rumpled stage curtain left to show he'd ever been there at all.

The police wizards looked relieved. "We have sent the troll to a forest far away from here," one of them announced with a bow to the audience. "He shouldn't bother the wizards and witches of Cacklewick any more."

Then there came a tremendous roar of applause, as the audience all began clapping and cheering.

"Three cheers for the brave little troll!" someone shouted, pointing at Oliver. "Hip hip…"

"HOORAY!" cheered the crowd.

"Hip hip…"

"HOORAY!"

"Hip hip…"

"HOORAY!"

"He my BROTHER," the Witch Baby
said loudly, and Oliver saw her and his
parents all beaming proudly at him.

After the cast had had a brief break to recover, the curtains opened once more and they went on with the play. When Oliver came back onstage as the troll, everyone stood up and applauded him all over again. He was quite glad to have his troll mask on to cover his blushes!

The rest of the play went off without a hitch, and Oliver really enjoyed being part of it. To think that he'd wanted to drop out, back when the parts had been announced! He was so glad he hadn't.

The best was yet to come, though. The next morning, *The Cacklewick Chronicle* thumped onto the doormat… and a scream of excitement went up from his mum.

There, on the front page, was a picture
of Oliver throwing the stage curtain over
the troll!

"Grunt, grunt!" said the Witch Baby when she saw it.

"There," said his mum proudly. "Didn't I say you were a hero?"

Oliver smiled at her, feeling very happy. She was right. Who said trolls couldn't be heroes, anyway?

The End

Oliver Moon
Junior Wizard

Collect all of Oliver Moon's magical adventures!

Oliver Moon and the Potion Commotion   ISBN 9780746073063
Can Oliver create a potion to win the Young Wizard of the Year award?

Oliver Moon and the Dragon Disaster   ISBN 9780746073070
Oliver's sure his new pet dragon will liven up the Festival of Magic...

Oliver Moon and the Nipperbat Nightmare   ISBN 9780746077917
Things go horribly wrong when Oliver gets to look after the school pet.

Oliver Moon's Summer Howliday   ISBN 9780746077924
Oliver suspects there is something odd about his hairy new friend, Wilf.

Oliver Moon's Christmas Cracker   ISBN 9780746077931
Can a special present save Oliver's Christmas at horrible Aunt Wart's?

Oliver Moon and the Spell-off   ISBN 9780746077948
Oliver must win a spell-off against clever Casper to avoid a scary forfeit.

Oliver Moon's Fangtastic Sleepover   ISBN 9780746084793
Will Oliver survive a school sleepover in the haunted house museum?

Oliver Moon and the Broomstick Battle   ISBN 9780746084809
Can Oliver beat Bully to win the Junior Wizards' Obstacle Race?

Happy Birthday, Oliver Moon   ISBN 9780746086872
Will Oliver's birthday party be ruined when his invitations go astray?

Oliver Moon and the Spider Spell   ISBN 9780746090749
Oliver's Grow-bigger spell lands the Witch Baby's pet in huge trouble.

Oliver Moon and the Troll Trouble   ISBN 9780746086865
Can Oliver save the show as the scary, stinky troll in the school play?

Oliver Moon and the Monster Mystery   ISBN 9780746090756
Strange things start to happen when Oliver wins a monster raffle prize...

All books are priced at £3.99